On the Night You Were Born

Nancy Tillman

FEIWEL AND FRIENDS

New York

On the night you were born,
the moon smiled with such wonder
that the stars peeked in to see you
and the night wind whispered,
"Life will never be the same."

Because there had never been anyone like you...
ever in the world.

A Special Book for You

_____

Love James + (Platters)
(Herb Reed + Platters)
Merry Christmas
2016

For you are fearfully and wonderfully made...

PSALMS 139

So enchanted with you were the wind and the rain
that they whispered the sound of your wonderful name.

The sound of your  name is a magical one.
Let's say it out loud before we go on.

It sailed through the farmland
high on the breeze...

Over the ocean...

And through the trees...

Until everyone heard it
and everyone knew
of the one and only ever you.

Not once had there been such eyes,
such a nose,
such silly, wiggly, wonderful toes.

In fact, I think I'll count to three
so you can wiggle your toes for me.

When the polar bears heard,
they danced until dawn.

From faraway places,
the geese flew home.

The moon stayed up until
morning next day.

And none of the ladybugs flew away.

So whenever you doubt just how special you are
and you wonder who loves you, how much and how far,
listen for geese honking high in the sky.
(They're singing a song to remember you by.)

Or notice the bears asleep at the zoo.
(It's because they've been dancing all night for you!)

Or drift off to sleep to the sound of the wind.
(Listen closely...it's whispering your name again!)

If the moon stays up until morning one day,
or a ladybug lands and decides to stay,
or a little bird sits at your window awhile,
it's because they're all hoping to see you smile...

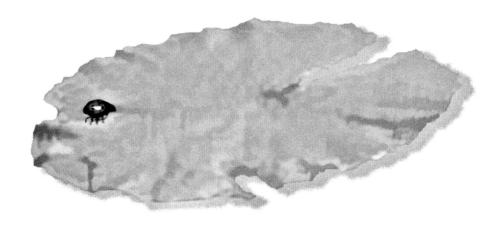

For never before in story or rhyme
(not even once upon a time)
has the world ever known a you, my friend,
and it never will, not ever again...

Heaven blew every trumpet
and played every horn
on the wonderful, marvelous
night you were born.

To Tucker and Tess, who are fearfully and wonderfully made.

A Feiwel and Friends Book
An Imprint of Macmillan

Feiwel and Friends books may be purchased for business or promotional use. For information on bulk purchases, please contact the Macmillan Corporate and Premium Sales Department at (800) 221-7945 x5442 or by e-mail at specialmarkets@macmillan.com.

Library of Congress Cataloging-in-Publication Data available

ISBN: 978-1-250-08395-1

Feiwel and Friends logo designed by Filomena Tuosto
First published in the United States by Darling Press LLC

First Feiwel and Friends Edition: 2006
10 9 8 7 6 5 4 3 2 1
mackids.com

Kohl's
Style: 1250083958
Factory Number: 123386
7/15-10/15

This special edition was printed for Kohl's Department Stores, Inc.
(for distribution on behalf of Kohl's Cares, LLC, its wholly owned subsidiary)
by Feiwel and Friends, an imprint of Macmillan Children's Book Group.

You are loved

Nancy Tillman is the author and illustrator of the bestselling picture books, *On the Night You Were Born*; its companion journal, *The Wonder of You: A Book for Celebrating Baby's First Year*; *You're Here for a Reason*; *The Heaven of Animals*; *Wherever You Are, My Love Will Find You*; *I'd Know You Anywhere, My Love*; *The Spirit of Christmas*; and *The Crown on Your Head*. She also created the mischievous cat Tumford in *Tumford the Terrible* and *Tumford's Rude Noises*, and illustrated *It's Time to Sleep, My Love* by Eric Metaxas.

Nancy's mission in creating her books is to convey to children everywhere that "You are loved." She lives in Portland, Oregon. You can visit her online at the Nancy Tillman Corner at mackids.com and at nancytillman.com.